# Note to parents, carers and teachers

*Read it yourself* is a series of modern stories, favourite characters and traditional tales written in a simple way for children who are learning to read. The books can be read independently or as part of a guided reading session.

Each book is carefully structured to include many high-frequency words vital for first reading. The sentences on each page are supported closely by pictures to help with understanding, and to offer lively details to talk about.

The books are graded into four levels that progressively introduce wider vocabulary and longer stories as a reader's ability and confidence grows.

## Ideas for use

- Begin by looking through the book and talking about the pictures. Has your child heard this story before?

- Help your child with any words he does not know, either by helping him to sound them out or supplying them yourself.

- Developing readers can be concentrating so hard on the words that they sometimes don't fully grasp the meaning of what they're reading. Answering the puzzle questions at the end of the book will help with understanding.

*For more information and advice on Read it yourself and book banding, visit* www.ladybird.com/readityourself

Book
Band
5

**Level 1** is ideal for children who have received some initial reading instruction. Each story is told very simply, using a small number of frequently repeated words.

## Special features:

chair

Daddy Pig

Peppa

Mummy Pig

Madame Gazelle

jumble sale

Opening pages introduce key story words

6

7

Large, clear type

"You can give this old chair, Daddy," says Peppa.

"No. This is a very good chair," says Daddy Pig.

12

13

Careful match between story and pictures

# Educational Consultant: Geraldine Taylor
# Book Banding Consultant: Kate Ruttle

LADYBIRD BOOKS

UK | USA | Canada | Ireland | Australia
India | New Zealand | South Africa

Ladybird Books is part of the Penguin Random House group of companies
whose addresses can be found at global.penguinrandomhouse.com.

www.penguin.co.uk   www.puffin.co.uk   www.ladybird.co.uk

Penguin
Random House
UK

Text adapted from Daddy Pig's Old Chair, first published by Ladybird Books, 2008
This version first published by Ladybird Books, 2014
005

This book is based on the
TV Series 'Peppa Pig'
'Peppa Pig' is created by
Neville Astley and Mark Baker
Peppa Pig © Astley Baker Davies Ltd/
Entertainment One UK Ltd, 2003

www.peppapig.com

Printed in China

A CIP catalogue record for this book is
available from the British Library

ISBN: 978–0–723–28050–7

MIX
Paper from
responsible sources
FSC® C018179

# Daddy Pig's
# Old Chair

Adaptation written by Ellen Philpott
Based on the TV series 'Peppa Pig'. 'Peppa Pig' is created
by Neville Astley and Mark Baker

chair

Peppa

Madame Gazelle

6

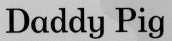
Daddy Pig

Mummy Pig

jumble sale

"We have to buy
a new school roof,"
says Madame Gazelle.
"We will have a jumble
sale to make money."

9

Peppa gives her toys to the jumble sale, to make money.

"I will give this toy, too," says Peppa.

11

"You can give this old chair, Daddy," says Peppa.

"No. This is a very good chair," says Daddy Pig.

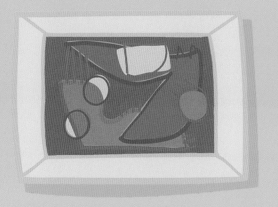

Peppa gives all the toys
to Madame Gazelle.

"You can have this old chair,
too," says Mummy Pig.

Peppa, Mummy Pig and
Daddy Pig go to the jumble
sale. Peppa's friends go, too.

Daddy's chair is at the
jumble sale. It looks
very old.

19

Peppa looks at all the toys
with her friends. Her old toy
looks very good.

"I will buy my old toy back," says Peppa.

All her friends buy their old toys back, too.

23

"I will buy this chair,"
says Daddy. "It will look
good with the old one."

"No. It IS the old one!"
says Mummy Pig.

"Oh. It was a lot of money,"
says Daddy Pig.

"Good," says Madame Gazelle. "We have made a lot of money. We can buy a new school roof!"

29

How much do you remember about Peppa Pig: Daddy Pig's Old Chair? Answer these questions and find out!

- Why is Madame Gazelle having a jumble sale?

- What does Peppa take to the jumble sale?

- What does Daddy Pig buy at the jumble sale?

# Look at the pictures from the story and say the order they should go in.

A

B

C

D

Answer: C, A, D, B.

# Read it yourself with Ladybird

## Tick the books you've read!

For children who are ready to take their first steps in reading.

**Level 1**

The Enormous Turnip · Fairy Friends · The Emperor's New Clothes · Cinderella · Goldilocks and the Three Bears · Topsy + Tim Go to the Zoo

Little Red Hen · The Magic Porridge Pot · Little Creatures · Recycling Fun! · The Princess and the Pea · Rex the Big Dinosaur · The Tale of Peter Rabbit · The Three Billy Goats Gruff

Why Giraffe has a Long Neck · The Ugly Duckling · Topsy + Tim At the Farm · The Big Pancake · Daddy Pig's Old Chair · THE RADISH ROBBER

For beginner readers who can read short, simple sentences with help.

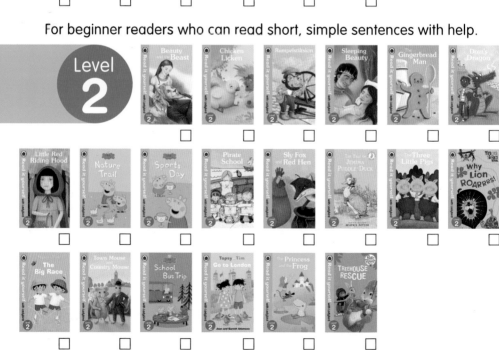

**Level 2**

Beauty and the Beast · Chicken Licken · Rumpelstiltskin · Sleeping Beauty · The Gingerbread Man · Dom's Dragon

Little Red Riding Hood · Nature Trail · Sports Day · Pirate School · Sly Fox and Red Hen · Jemima Puddle-Duck · The Three Little Pigs · Why Lion ROARRRS!

The Big Race · Town Mouse and Country Mouse · School Bus Trip · Topsy + Tim Go to London · The Princess and the Frog · TREEHOUSE RESCUE

 Available on the App Store

The Read it yourself with Ladybird app is now available

 ANDROID APP ON Google play

App also available on Android™ devices